SWEET DREAMS

This book has been made possible in part by the New York State Council of the Arts, the Leslie Scalapino - O Books Fund, and donations from Belladonna* supporters. Belladonna* is a proud member of the Community of Literary Magazines and Presses.

Library of Congress Cataloging-in-Publication Data

Names: Sneed, Pamela, author.
Title: Sweet dreams / Pamela Sneed.
Description: Brooklyn, New York : Belladonna Collaborative, [2018] |
Series: Akilah Oliver Series
Identifiers: LCCN 2017028379 | ISBN 9780988539990 (acid-free paper)
Classification: LCC PS3569.N34 S94 2018 | DDC 813/.54--dc23
LC record available at https://lccn.loc.gov/2017028379

Cover Art: Pamela Sneed
Book Design: Yanyi
Author Photo (back cover): Patricia Silva

Published by Belladonna* Collaborative

SWEET DREAMS

Pamela Sneed

INTRODUCTION BY GREGG BORDOWITZ

POSTSCRIPT BY THE AUTHOR

BELLADONNA* COLLABORATIVE

BROOKLYN

2018

Introduction

Pamela Sneed's considerable body of writing and her growing literature is a unique testament to the writer's engagement with liberation struggles—the writer's own personal story as it is entwined in the larger currents of historical trajectories. Sneed incorporates the representations of adjacent and related movements in all forms of popular culture. Her writing is an ongoing chronicle of the senses. It is not simply imaginary or projective, nor a cerebral encounter, although the writer's mind is ever-active on the page. Sneed feels her way around stories and their kindred relation to fellow travelers. It's an account that includes the internal motion of cells, synapses, and sensations, directly felt by the body of a ruminating subject and a responsible witness. All information is available to the writer's craft as it passes through the various pronouns and positions, through poetry and prose, quotation and testimony, accumulating to one powerful liturgy chronicling the tests and triumphs of a survivor.

Sweet Dreams is a work of extraordinary erudition. Here, Sneed goes Talmudic on a huge corpus of knowledge drawn from literature, poetry, movies, and life experience. The self is a composite of inspirations, inherited legends, and the "I" is a roving reporter collecting her story through attachments. This work recounts pilgrimages of multiple selves and a singular self. Not a contradiction. The writer is the subject, the witness, the protagonist, and the scholar; a performer, a preacher, a freedom fighter, an artist. All these aspects are present through temporalities arising, relating, transforming within the capacious intellect of a brilliant writer. The work calls to mind a disparate number of authors such as Kathy Acker, Severo Sarduy, and Christopher Isherwood.

Consider the work in geological terms. Layers of silt carried by mountain rivers become mineral to replenish the landscape, become rock, minerals, gems, glass; the various shapes of glass and the reflections in varied surfaces; or hundreds of shattered uniform pieces of windshield strewn across the pavement. *Sweet Dreams* mines glittering flashing pixels across many screens refreshing at varying rates. Add to that thick vinyl and the diamond stylus. Revolutions per minute, rates of velocity, all calculations tabulated in this testimony accrue with impact, verve, intensities. All on the page.

Switching to another descriptive metaphor—*Sweet Dreams* is a manifold work of exquisite origami. With each fold the elements of the story are carefully worked and shaped out of one substance to achieve a singular beautiful form.

Gregg Bordowitz
October 25, 2017

Sweet Dreams

In many ways, I am fortunate to have always had a strong sense of identity. As a poet, performer, professor, I am someone who leads, whom people look up to, emulate, compete with, steal from, and in more cases than cared to report, tear down. Like recent victims of police brutality, and heinous crimes enacted historically and presently against women, I have been viewed by some with fear and contempt. In the words of the late great poet Sekou Sundiata, "It all depends on the skin, it all depends on the skin you're living in." Sometimes I laugh and view myself as someone accused of practicing sorcery in an African Village or, in a not-so-funny scenario, accused and persecuted like witches in Salem, Massachusetts. As a 6ft 2½in dark Black Lesbian with a shaved head, my identity provokes many reactions, just by being in a room.

I want to go back to the idea of being stolen from as that's an ongoing part of my experience.

My earliest sense of identity came from a Black woman in Boston. She was dark-skinned with a shaved head and during the summer months she drove a jeep convertible down Huntington Avenue, one of the most prominent avenues in Boston, near Northeastern University. It was the '80s. I was best friends with talk show host Wendy Williams. We attended

Northeastern University. You have to understand how conservative Boston was. It is a city famous for The Bunker Hill Monument, the statue of Paul Revere. It is also famous for being provincial, with red cobblestone streets, row after row of brownstones, deep racial division, and its '70s bussing scandals that attempted to desegregate White city schools with Black kids from the inner-city. It was ugly, with White people with contorted faces who spat on Black kids, carried signs and shouted, "Niggers Go Home." So you have to understand, a Black woman with a shaved head driving down the most prominent avenue in Boston in a jeep convertible with the top down was unheard of. I was 18 years old and saw her sometimes from the window of an apartment I lived in on Huntington Avenue. Even with my limited scope coming from the suburbs, she was an image of beauty and perfection to me.

Wendy Williams and I met through a program at Northeastern for African American students. It was a program created probably in the late '60s or '70s to aid in the retention of Black students who didn't have great grades in high school. It was called Projective Ujima named after a principle of Kwanzaa: collective work and responsibility. Most of the staff were women involved in Civil Rights and they wore dashikis. The most prominent administrator was Verdaya, who saw I was open and spent lots of time talking to me about Black Power.

I became immersed in the Institute, Wendy stayed clear of it. I don't think I'd ever seen any Black woman who ever looked like Wendy and spoke like her. She was golden-colored brown, wore red red lipstick with her outlined lips. Her brown hair had blonde highlights. She was heavy set and big boned. She considered herself to be a valley girl, or an African-American Princess. She was wealthy. In her dorm room all of her accessories were pink, her favorite color at the time. There were a few boxes of Gaultier that were black and white striped. He was her favorite designer and she was obsessed with his cologne. She only wore labels and Izod shirts in bright colors like pink. She only drank Orange Crush soda from a can, and she only sipped it through a straw. That was Wendy. I suppose we both connected because we were outsiders. We were both studying Communications.

Wendy went into radio. I can say she was pretty much the same person then as she is now: frank, brash, smart, outspoken. I followed Wendy everywhere. She was very into men; I wasn't. Wendy really liked a guy from a Black fraternity. Fraternities were popular on campus. He was a Q. The Qs were the bad guy fraternity on campus. They were jocks. Many got in on sports scholarships and had limited abilities to read and write. Their colors were purple and gold. Having opportunity to watch these guys in a step show was truly exhilarating—how they went from lumbering to agile, dancers playing ancient rhythms on their bodies. One night I went with Wendy to visit the Q fraternity House. She wanted to hook up with one of her favorite Qs. I ended up in a separate room with some guy I didn't like much and was kind of forced to have sex with. It was a compromising situation and I don't think I've ever mentioned it until now.

I also sometimes hung out with my younger cousin from the suburbs. She visited me on campus. She, Wendy and I were a trio. We once went to visit Wendy's parent's house in New Jersey. It was a mansion. I don't think I'd ever encountered such wealth. I met her Dad, a handsome light-skinned man. We met in his study; it was a library full of books against the wall. "He's a writer," Wendy told us. The way she said *writer*, it was full of reverence and respect. He might have been the first sign of things to come for me. During that visit Wendy, my cousin, and I went to NYC and snuck into an infamous club, The Paradise Garage. It required us getting fake IDs because you had to be a member and be at least 21. My younger cousin, Lesa, had too much to drink from the punch bowl, infamously filled with tabs of acid and red fruit punch. She'd passed out near the bathroom and my life as a young person depended on reviving her—if I, we, didn't, we were in big trouble. I finally did.

Wendy and I had united in that we were both wild cards. In Boston, we went to parties, I started taking her to Gay parties. Before I was ready and willing to face it, she declared, "Oh my god Pam, You're going to be a Lesbian." She also proceeded to out me to Northeastern's Black basketball team, whom we were both friends with. She went around campus telling them, "You know, Pam's a Lesbian." She and I separated over that. I never followed her career and fame on the radio so much, but every so often, years after Northeastern, in New York, friends would call me and say, "Wendy Williams talked about you on the radio today." Wendy would say, "The only Lesbian I know is Pamela Sneed."

In the early 2000s, I ran into Wendy. She was working still at WBLS. I was bartending. She came in and we talked. She was outrageous. First thing she said, was, "Hey Pam do you want to see my liposuction," and pulled up her shirt moderately to show the orange peel skin. She went on, "My parents wanted me to marry an A-lister/Ivy league man, but this is the type of man I like," and she pulled out a photo of a man that looked to me like a mug shot. I smiled politely. I told her I was writing a book. In response, she said, “Anyone can write a book.” At the end of our conversation she said, “I don’t have many women friends.” And in a moment, as if all the years between us hadn’t passed, as if perhaps beneath fame, there might be loneliness, she asked, “Would you like to have dinner with me sometime, Pam?” I’m not sure if I answered. I understand many years ago she wrote a tell-all about her origins. She said in college she had a roommate that was a Lesbian. I imagine the Lesbian alluded to was me.

Shortly after my friendship with Wendy in Boston, I fell in love with a White woman who was a punk rocker. She looked like Marilyn Monroe, but kept one side of her hair long, the other shaved, had pale skin and wore bright red lipstick. She introduced me to thrift store shopping. Once a month we filled garbage bags of vintage clothes for $1.00. Her name was Lauren and, when introduced by a mutual former boyfriend, she turned to me and said of me, “She’s beautiful.” At the outset, we admired each other’s clothes and style, though mine was a little less developed. The day we met I wore a white leather mini-skirt. When I moved from Huntington Avenue, sort of off-campus housing for Northeastern, Lauren and I quickly lived together as roommates. It was clear Lauren was the older leader though she was only 23; she lived in the city and had a great wardrobe. From her, like what happens on talk shows, I was getting a makeover. In the beginning she was generous and we wore matching complementing outfits comprised of thrift store finds and her extensive wardrobe, then something changed. After numerous infractions of sneaking into her room to borrow her holey wool sweaters, pencil skirts and vintage glamour, I was forbidden from wearing her clothes. She was the epitome of cool, and I guess I'd been caught trying to steal her identity. I don't remember many of Lauren's words or the conversations between us, only the day I'd told her I loved her. We sat outside on the sidewalk of Gracie's. Gracie was a dark Black man with a shaved head who wore a bowtie and owned a thrift store. "I love you," I said.

Like water in the Bahamas, it was clear, I could see all the way down to the bottom... silver schools of fish.

"I love you too," she said.

"No," I said, "I love you," placing emphasis on love and not as friends. Like a wobbly colt separated from its mother, I was determined, pushed myself up and forced myself to stand for the first time.

Lauren and I lived platonically on Peterborough St. behind Fenway Park, the famous home of the Boston Red Sox, a conservative baseball team. Lauren didn't consider herself to be a Lesbian. Pop-star Annie Lennox had just released the song *Sweet Dreams Are Made of This.* There was a huge life-sized poster of her album cover at the bus stop near our house. Her hair was cropped, dyed orange/fire engine red. She wore red lipstick in contrast to pale skin. She wore a pinstriped men's suit. In today's terms she'd be a drag king or cross-dresser. She held a pointer as if in school and a teacher. Again it was the early '80s and there was freedom in her style. It was radical then to see a woman on a bus stop in Boston publicly dressed as a man as much as it was seeing a Black woman with a shaved head. It was this pop star, these moments, and all of these people who paved the way for me to leave Boston and transfer from Northeastern. I knew I'd wanted to write, and I'd heard about a school in the West Village. It was Sonya, a Northeastern friend who told me about The New School over dinner one day. "It's a small school and you can write." At that time, writing sounded like magic and I was drawn to it. Sonya and I reconnected a few years ago on Facebook, we hadn't spoken since the Northeastern years. She was a dark dark brown, almost black in skin tone, a beautiful woman. She said, "Pam girl, you gave me the courage to wear bright lipstick. You said bright lipstick was ok on dark skin." She said, "From that day on, I never wore dark lipstick." I hadn't remembered that at all. I suppose both Lauren and Annie Lennox's lipstick tips had helped liberate me and Sonya.

At Sonya's urging, I made an appointment for an interview at The New School. I travelled to New York and met a White woman with a short buzz cut who showed me around campus. At that time, the New School/ Seminar College Campus was two blocks on 11th Street and 12th Street. Ray's Pizza on 6th Avenue, a smoke shop on the corner of 11th, and sometimes a church on 5th Avenue where graduation was held and Sekou Sundiata dedicated a poem to me. The New School was beautiful to me, exotic like the land of America that immigrants imagine with streets lined with gold. An adult student, a Black woman from Haiti, told me once that she literally believed the streets of America were lined with gold and it was always warm. She said, "I showed up at Kennedy airport with no family/no contacts in the dead of winter with no coat and no going back..." At Northeastern I flunked out of journalism twice before switching my major to Communications. I only remember a wretched skinny white man who announced at the beginning of journalism class,

"Most of you aren't going to make it. It's my job to weed you out." It was daunting. At that time, I didn't understand the concept of creative writing. If one wanted to write, one became a journalist.

When I was a child, a little Black girl just learning to articulate, I said, "I want to be a stewardess when I grow up." I imagined wearing a form-fitting suit with the winged signature pin of Pan Am airlines on the lapel. Pan Am was popular then and that was the line of work and the glamorous future offered to little Black girls. Through that program at the African American Institute, I learned about poetry and Black consciousness. Black professors spoke nostalgically of the '60s and of an Africa where there were Kings and Queens. On the plus side, the Institute and Project Ujima held many variety shows and art events that I became involved in. I became sort of its star. I remember a packed auditorium where I sat on the edge of a stage with my legs crossed. I had written a poem for Black History Month and I said, "Come follow a dream to a mountaintop," referencing MLK Jr. On the downside, the Institute was homophobic. I wrote a story once but have since lost it about the time the Black Student Union brought Minister Louis Farrakhan of the Nation of Islam to speak. The hall was packed with more Black students than I had ever seen on campus. He said, specifically, after imitating a Gay man, "If you're Gay, you won't get into the kingdom of heaven." He then did something theatrical and wiggled around and pranced on stage imitating his rendition of a Gay man. The room erupted, stood on its feet and clapped wildly. At the time I was far from myself and can't recall if I stood and clapped too. Though homophobic, it was the African American Institute at Northeastern with its Black faculty and Black is Beautiful slogans that later gave me courage and language to confront the New School's race and diversity problem. There were only three Black students at Seminar College and not one person of color on the faculty. It was me and some radical white students who helped integrate the college and, after some trial and error, brought the Poet Sekou Sundiata to the faculty, but that's another story.

Before this, in a memorable scene, I went home to my father and told him of my plans to leave Boston. In a tiny apartment's kitchen, he stood at the sink with his back to me. I announced, "I'm moving to New York, Dad." My father contemplated for a moment, and turned to look at me.

If this were a painting, I imagine that in the room with my father and I were Wendy, Lauren, Martin Luther King, The African American Institute, Verdaya, Annie Lennox, Sonya, and the mysterious Black woman who drove down Huntington Ave. with a shaved head.

Without missing a beat, like a minister giving the benediction or blessing at a sermon's end, he said, "If that's what you want, I won't stop you, Pamela."

Shortly after, I bought a one-way 30-dollar airline ticket from Boston to New York. I left on an airline called People's Express. Standing at the gate, my father waved goodbye. Like the scene at the end of a touching film, where lifelong partners separate and one wants to pursue their destiny, I turned around for a last look. You know the scene where one partner stands on the top step entering a train car, while the other is on the platform watching as the train leaves the station... Or in the film *The Bodyguard* when Kevin Costner's character is in an airfield looking up at his love, played by Whitney Houston, before she boards the plane, which will make its ascent toward heaven. In ways my father and I were both letting go of everything we had. I was saying goodbye to the apartment I grew up in on Bowdoin St. in Malden, Mass., which was just a few steps away and two tiers above a housing project and just a few blocks away before it was sold from my grandmother's house with its back porch, sometimes overgrown backyard, and summer garden with collard greens—that small town feel where everyone knew each other.

There's a story by Amy Tan in *The Joy Luck Club* that I teach to my students. It is rife with themes of letting go, loss, freedom, and survival. I'm paraphrasing, but the narrator says, "My mother lost all she had leaving China for America, her husband, her twin daughters, but she never looked back with regret." I think about this story with regard to the sacrifices some people are forced to make in pursuit of a new life. A few years ago, my father was sitting in his favorite chair at the kitchen table. I was visiting. I'm not sure what prompted it, but he said, "You never gave me any problems. You made your own decisions, once you chose your path that was it, you stayed on it."

On my first day at The New School/Lang College, I showed up with an ounce of pure cocaine from a Columbian drug dealer. He'd urged me to distribute it amongst my peers. I attended freshman orientation. I met the drug dealer in New York. He was the brother of a friend from Boston who'd connected us. I paid 700 dollars and stayed at his high-rise on 57th St. His name was Alberto. He was only there intermittently. I can only remember him saying things like, "Pamela don't eat butter, it'll ruin your body." Once I moved, I never saw him again, but here I was on the first day of The New School getting high with two other freshmen: a white boy from Switzerland named Jerome, who had curly black hair, and Elizabeth, a white punk rocker girl with a shaved head who wore combat boots. Besides meeting teachers, Elizabeth and I spent most of the day snorting cocaine in the Women's room stall. No matter what you said, every sentence of Elizabeth's ended with, "Yeah man." I'm not sure if she and I kissed on that day but there was an attraction. I think I believed meeting Elizabeth was an omen and, almost immediately after meeting her and moving to New York, modeling myself after the Black woman in Boston, I shaved my head. I found a friend I knew from the club days in Boston to do it. We sat in her kitchen. She used a straight-edge razor. The first result looked harsh, like the singer Isaac Hayes, only I was a woman. I supplemented by wearing lots of lipstick. This is back before women actually did this. You have to understand it was the '80s and I could have been murdered for that type of thing. This is when people cruised the West Village to gay bash queers, and women who were brazen in their identity were victims too. I'm thinking about a young Black Lesbian named Sakia Gunn who was murdered on the street in Newark for her queerness. Dreadlocks on Black people had also been the issue of the day. The hairstyle was perceived then as unclean, a mark of militancy. Looming in the background was what happened to MOVE in Philadelphia, the Back to Africa group that wore dreadlocks and were targeted and bombed in broad daylight. It was a Black Mayor who orchestrated the attack. 11 people died, 5 were children, and 66 homes in the predominately Black neighborhood were burnt down.

At the New School I was sitting with a woman professor who taught War and Women's Writing. Another famous woman professor sat in on our meeting. At that time, The New School was still famous for liberalism and housing intellectuals in exile, those who spoke out against governments for certain unpopular ideals. Without much language to express it, I felt frustrated by the ideas of White middle class feminism at the New School. I couldn't see myself or anything like me in stories by much heralded heroines Tillie Olsen or Doris Lessing. Also, there were only two other Black students besides myself, and one rarely attended class. For my first year at The New School I didn't speak. I realize now it was shock. Mainly, the students at The New School were white, upper middle class, and they spoke to me in a language I imagined then as hieroglyphics. They ate sushi and brown rice. It wasn't until Sekou Sundiata declared in class one day "Black people speak two languages" that I understood my dilemma, and it freed me. I started to speak.

I wrote a paper about what I imagined Black feminism to be. I had moved to a poor neighborhood/the projects in Harlem; after the high-rise, that too was shocking. I had never experienced the dense poverty. I stayed with a Black woman with three kids. It was a friend's mother from Northeastern. Every day there were smells of piss and feces in the hallway. There was glass on the playgrounds. I talked about a Black woman who had to raise her children in poverty and endure these things. I talked about her youngest daughter, Naima, with long black braids and deep brown skin whom I often babysat, who was 8 or 9 and never allowed to play outdoors because it was too dangerous. I talked about myself, how walking amongst the idle boys in an isolated part of Manhattan en-route to the subway, at 6ft 2½in with a shaved head, was like walking a gauntlet. I also wore vintage and thrift store glamour influenced by my Boston days. Every morning I was hazed by those idle young men with words like faggot, skinhead, dyke. I was never sure if those threats would end in violence. I can only imagine my determination and my style acted as some sort of bulletproof vest, because I never changed to fit in. AIDS had just begun to emerge then. It was at the apartment in Harlem, I opened up the Daily News and saw an ominous headline in black letters announcing "A Gay Plague" described as "God's curse on Homosexuals." They were closing bathhouses to stop men from having sex. At that time, I didn't recognize myself fully as a Lesbian, but it was there, with this new plague and the hatred of homosexuals hovering over us and in the background like fear. I never talked about it.

My paper on the Black woman in Harlem had been late, so I ending up reading to the two famous White feminists in a conference. After I read, one got up and danced around the cubicle and spoke/sang in the most melodious voice, "She's a writer! She's a writer!" In a tiny office on 12th St. with a library of books against the wall, those two women squatted and gave birth to me. Another pivotal moment came through an internship. I met two Women of Color drummers. They were Lesbians. I invited them to The New School to perform. "We will come to perform, only if you recite poetry," one of the drummers said. I went on stage with them and recited poetry. The lights went on. I received a standing ovation. I was born, would never again go back to the girl I was from Boston. I was a poet and performer who was 6ft 2½in, brazen and outspoken with a shaved head.

I want to point out the earliest parts of my identity and how it was formed, because I've known better than most a little of who I was at an early age. This awareness has been both challenging, rewarding, and has provided conditions for many setbacks. In another story, I mention Mrs. Carrington, a very thin, spindly Black woman with light brown skin, who was a school guidance counselor. In 4th grade, I'd been in trouble for fighting, the same year I started writing. I was sent to Mrs. Carrington, the second of two Black women I'd ever meet in my entire early education. I didn't want Mrs. Carrington. I wanted the other guidance counselor, a heavy-set older White man who was always seen through a glass office window playing chess and checkers with students. I was sent to Ms. Carrington. I imagine her job was to analyze my problems and help me with them. I imagine the conversation started something like, "Hello dear, how are you today?" I can't imagine I talked much about my family life, but Mrs. Carrington, either through experience or training, diagnosed my problem as identity. She was the first woman to ever look at me with kind eyes, and instead of an expected reprimand for fighting. She gave me two books about Black people: one was the *Egypt Game*; I don't remember its content only pictures. The other book was about Harriet Tubman, called *Runaway Slave.* I read that book over and over from cover to cover. The first few lines began, "Can human beings be owned the way chickens, dogs, cows can?" I'm grateful to Mrs. Carrington because *Runaway Slave* saved my life. The first book I gained acclaim for as an adult was loosely based on Harriet Tubman, and so the great conductor who freed slaves has stayed with me all of my life. Like the character Celie in *The Color Purple* who addresses God in her journal, every journal entry I have ever written has been addressed "Dear Harriet," to Harriet Tubman. In almost every story/poem I have ever written she appears, weaving her way through my trials, setbacks and tribulations. She leads me through the woods. There's a story in my mind I would one day like to see realized—I always imagine it as a screenplay—a contemporary story of a young Black girl who is abused. She disappears into her room and reads *Runaway Slave*. Through a time capsule in her closet she is transported to the time of Harriet Tubman. She gets to witness the famous conductor on her journeys to free slaves. She is educated on slavery. She witnesses Harriet's story and heroism.

In Sherman Alexie's *The Absolutely True Diary of a Part-Time Indian*, the main character Junior is sort of a bullied teen. Near the end, in a moment of success, he is playing basketball and makes the basket. The narrator says (I'm paraphrasing): "If you believe, at that moment, I was lifted on my ancestors' shoulders." So I guess, too, if you believe, in all of my moments of success it's Harriet herself who lifts me and whose shoulders I stand on.

Shortly before I was sent to the guidance counselor for fighting, I wrote my first story at age nine. It was about a gypsy. I was an only child, an avid reader, loved sci-fi and had a vivid imagination, which is how I survived. I brought it to school and showed my teachers and they said it was impossible for me to have written it. Implied was that it was far beyond my years in scope and also, that I was a little Black girl for whom, I assume, expectations were low. I was pulled out into the hallway by two teachers to discuss it. "Did someone help you?" they asked. "No, I wrote it myself," I said. They exchanged looks of disbelief. "Someone must have helped you write it, who was it?" And our exchange went on for a while until they gave up, refusing to believe me. I attribute writing the story to when I was eight and heard an infomercial on TV for Maya Angelou's audiocassette. If I recall it, she was reciting a few lines of "And Still I Rise." I was riveted. Hearing just the few lines of a poem blew open the windows and doors to my consciousness. Her poetry and voice planted a seed. People today in poetry circles talk about how good or bad a poet Maya Angelou was, but if she were alive today like my guidance counselor Mrs. Carrington, I would go to them both and say *thank you*. Thank you for saving me, for saving this Black girl's life.

Recently, I was in a conference with a university student who said she'd never written poetry before. We spoke over the phone. Her work was very beautiful and I said in an impromptu moment, "Read it to me." I wanted her to hear herself and how beautiful it was. She started to cry.

When I was 18 or 19 years old at Northeastern, I took an acting class with a very liberal/hippie-ish type White woman. I was asked to present a final scene. I found a Black playwright and the scene involved a White boy, so I enlisted a classmate. I directed the scene. At the end of it, my character asks, "Does anyone know what time it is?" When I finished the Professor asked, "Who helped you?" I said, "No one." She said, "It is impossible; you could never have directed that scene." She and I did bond. We actually became friends, but she never believed me. I was talking to her over the phone and she said, "I'm going to help you. I'm going to make sure you get into an acting conservatory." She forgot her promise and I don't think I ever followed up. I do think that conservatory might have changed my life's path, made it easier. In that same conversation, I confided in her and told her I was smoking a lot of pot. She said, "If you want to be an actress you can't smoke pot. You'll have no memory." From that day on, I stopped smoking pot. I did other things, but never pot.

From the story that I'd written when I was nine, and from these teachers and their responses, I learned I was gifted, almost supernaturally. Looking back, it was this knowledge that was the balloon carrying me through most of my life.

As an aside, I sometimes envy actress Lupita Nyong'o, the dark Black girl with closely cropped hair who was the breakout star of the film *12 Years a Slave.* I think what about all the Lupitas, me and all the beautiful dark Black girls when the world wasn't ready for people like us. If maybe I'd gone to a conservatory for acting, I might have been a breakthrough Lupita, only it would have been in the '80s. I said this to a friend while we were driving. I also sighed in the same breath as if answering my own question. "Well then, I guess I wouldn't have become a freedom fighter and that's really my life's path."

So I have had an early sense of my identity, and I'm not sure where and how it fits in, but as an adult I began to reject myself, reject my person, my goodness, my worth.

My most formative experience as a child was when my father first married my stepmother. I was six years old, and I describe that experience comedically in a poem as her figure appearing like a monstrous shadow on a white wall, and right as the victim/me is devoured, I turn to face the camera, frozen in death. There is also something in this poem about Carrie, the girl from a horror film who is supernaturally gifted and begins, after much degradation and abuse, to use her power. From the beginning my stepmother made it clear she didn't want me and that I was something that came, regrettably, with the package called my father. She also passed for White, along with most of her 12 brothers and sisters. As a young Black girl, I represented some of my stepmother's deepest issues. Though poor, she grew up in very middle class suburbs and would say, "Black girls didn't like me as a child, they were jealous of mine and my sisters' long hair." Early in her marriage to my father, some of her family members came to visit. They had school age children and we all went out to play. We stayed out past sunset. When we returned, my stepmother was furious and assumed I had led them into being late to return. It wasn't actually my choice, but I'd been singled out. That's the first day I remember negativity being attached to me that wasn't mine. Later there were other moments. The seams of a mattress that I slept on were fraying. When I came home, my stepmother accused, "You've destroyed that mattress," although I hadn't touched it. It was an excuse to grab my father's long black belt and administer severe lashes. Again, something was attached to me that I didn't do. This was a pattern established in my life early on. One of my first jobs at a Queer youth agency treated me terribly after a while. I remember telling someone about it. "You were a scapegoat," she said. Because this was such a pattern, and there was rarely anyone to counteract this information about me, I myself believed it was true. In my adult life, in relationships, time after time I was blamed. There was a story attached to me that I could not escape. In the film *Bowfinger*, Eddie Murphy plays an actor where people place him in their movie, project and weave a story around him and he's not even there, has never agreed to it. He's not at all aware that every action he makes is being filmed. In one scenario, someone once asked me, "Why didn't you stand up for yourself? Why didn't you say something?" and I replied because no matter what I said or did I knew the person couldn't see me. What lingers for me are the scars—knowledge that if I were a

White woman or man, or fair-skinned, straight or rich, none of these things would be attached to me.

As an adult, my rejection manifested in overworking, hiding, and tremendous fear, fear of being seen. For years, I trembled uncontrollably at the slightest provocation. I'm thinking about Audre Lorde here, the paradox expressed at each of us as human beings so desperately wants to be seen also, that visibility is often the source of our greatest fear. Oh fear. Oh fear. I could write volumes about fear, about the time I was working on a play and the director said, as if cutting to the chase and all the monologues and rehearsals couldn't solve it, "Your greatest obstacle is fear." I think for some reason about the AIDS crisis in the late '80s and early '90s, watching friends die and there it was in their eyes, FEAR, the most horrible and barbaric fear. It had talons and wings and bore its fangs into each of us. It bled out veins. It lurked in corners, in broad daylight. It was grey with barbed wire fences. It was parasitic... I've been thinking recently about a performance I did, how I feel an incredible power where once there was only fear. I haven't mentioned all the work it took to get here, all the therapy, writing, teaching, performances, and the tremendous failures. It's like a prisoner who chisels through a wall for years with only a small tool or icepick, like a slave who makes years and years of attempts to run away and finally, if their spirit or body hasn't completely broken, succeeds.

I'm a great believer in therapy, have done it for years, and that's had its ups and downs, like the one time I needed a therapist and I met a woman who took my insurance through the Screen Actors Guild, and she asked at first meeting, "How long have you been a man?" I said, "I'm not a man." She asked me another time, "When do you want to talk about your transition?" Sadly, I really needed to talk with her because I was being harassed in an MFA program I attended. I stayed for a while, even though sometimes when I was talking she fell asleep, or when I got long-winded she'd say, "Hurry up." Another time in therapy, I started seeing a White man who kept asking me about coming out as a Lesbian when it wasn't what I had gone to talk about. He then asked me about my sexual practices, "Any Bondage? Sadomasochism?" I was aghast. I had a Black woman therapist for ten years and had never talked about intimate sexual practices. After all the many therapists, I've finally met Natasha, a White Jewish woman who is the mother I never had, who believes in me, listens, encourages me, and when sometimes I'm desperate to know the outcome, she offers the one thing I've always longed for but never received from a lover or friend: "We're in this together." It's as if after having suffered something like a stroke or paralysis she stays with me on the long road to recovery, applauds each step, helps me walk. In 1992, when I last saw Audre Lorde alive at the "I Am Your Sister" Conference in Boston, she walked out onto the stage, spread wings of her dashiki to embrace and engulf us all, we seekers of knowledge and justice. Of her battle with cancer she declared, "I began on this journey as a coward."

I see the transformation of my own cowardice into strength. I know when you conquer fear, it's like being on a mountaintop. You can see everything. It's like Leonardo DiCaprio's character in the film *Blood Diamond. Blood Diamond* is about the corrupt diamond trade in Sierra Leone during the 1990s civil war. Leonardo DiCaprio plays a white mercenary and Dimon Hounsou plays a Black fisherman. Both men's lives are transformed when Hounsou finds a rare diamond. DiCaprio, a grifter, tries to steal it. *Blood Diamond* reminds me of a film called *The Defiant Ones* made in 1958. It is a black-and-white film starring Tony Curtis and Sidney Poitier, both fugitives who escape a chain gang. They are on the run but shackled together. It is a dance and a deep allegory about race, on how the fate of one race depends upon the fate of the other. It is like Athol Fugard's *The Blood Knot* written at the height of apartheid where two brothers, one Black and one white are engaged in a struggle but linked inextricably by blood. At the end of *Blood Diamond* the two adversaries have become friends. DiCaprio's character is fatally wounded. Symbolically, he lays on a mountaintop, dying. Through his journey, his eyes have been opened. Perhaps he sees Hounsou now as a brother. He hands back the rare pink diamond he has tried to steal. Seeing DiCaprio giving up, his body giving way, Hounsou offers, "I can carry you." DiCaprio responds "No," and then says, resonant of the battle between races, of the blood spill, of the part he's played as white man in stealing, "No More."

It echoes and resounds like the sermons of the preachers I grew up with, who shouted of sorrow and pain and suffering and a day when there is and will be "No More." I wrote as an adult a poem and performed it in the voice of a preacher delivering a sermon, a person who has transcended fear, from the perspective taking of a plane ride, "Passing over, tumultuous water, from the sky, mountains look like ant hills and cities torches of candlelight."

Oh oh, there is something I remember Harry Belafonte said. He was friends with Martin Luther King. I'm paraphrasing, but he said Martin Luther King had a small twitch in his eye for a long time. One day it was gone and Harry asked him, "Martin what happened? Why has your eye stopped twitching?' and Martin replied, " Because, I no longer fear death."

There is a story I've always kept in my heart by Reverend Zachary Jones who preached in New York at Unity Fellowship. He was speaking of flying and transcendence and said to the congregation as inspiration, "An eagle has a wing span of 30ft. I said, an eagle has a wing span of 30ft, so what are you doing on the ground with chickens?!"

I was working on a play once with a dancer and she looked at my long arms outstretched and she said, "My God, Pamela, your wing span."

As for my self-rejection, there was a structure already in place. I had been rejected by birth parents who placed me into adoption in Boston. All I know is that they were students. He was dark, 6ft 4in. She was 5ft 10in. They were from Virginia. The first fiction I ever wrote in College took place in Virginia. The people who adopted me then divorced. I went with my father, and my adoptive mother never returned to retrieve me. My third mother whom my father married had psychological problems. My adopted father stayed, but disappeared into depression and alcohol. And so I began as an adult a process of cutting, self-mutilation, where inside I began to reject myself, my beauty, my strength, my worth, the work I'd done. I suppose it's what an anorexic describes as a process of disappearing. I thought things would be better if I weren't around. I dropped out of performance, dating, everything. I remember some years back when I was talking to someone, venting about something as I often did then, he was shocked and said, "This isn't you." He was right. It wasn't. Then I was left to ponder by myself how I could develop and spend more than 40 years in a persona that was not mine.

I heave tears as I write this.

Self-rejection and self-battering.

At the New School, in my first fiction class, I wrote about a Black dyke who sang blues, cross-dressed like Big Mama Thorton, Annie Lennox before her, wore men's clothes and in essence was a runaway slave.

In the beginning, in the prologue, I wrote:

> *Every woman she'd ever known had been harnessed and broken.*

Wanting to escape this fate, at the end of the prologue I wrote:

> *In life, there are moments*
>
> *for which all drafts prepare you*
>
> *love tested, failed*
>
> *songs sung and unsung*
>
> *when disparate ends tie together and vision*

like purpose comes clear

Joe, a piss poor Black bulldagger, disappeared

and left no note.

There are a few things I remember from that novel, when the small town Joe lives in betrays her, and the church members oust her for being a Lesbian. The names on the paper asking for her departure were all people she'd loved or helped. After Joe disappears down an unlit road, an analogy to that tumultuous path slaves forged in pursuit of freedom, I wrote:

> *Like all families when the wars for acceptance were over, they would miss the man's hat, denim coveralls, and women's feet stuffed in work boots.*

The background for this story is that I grew up watching my stepmother beaten mercilessly. Among many things I saw her continuously dragged up and down flights of stairs in an apartment building we lived in.

Given my history, you have to understand how seeing that dark Black woman with a shaved head driving down Huntington Avenue in a jeep convertible was the first image of freedom I'd ever known.

To see my stepmother beaten by my father that way was difficult to say the least. The most memorable beating came after she returned from the doctor's office, and the doctor noticed her body covered in black and blue marks. He said, and I wrote about this in my signature piece *Imagine Being More Afraid of Freedom Than Slavery*, "You'll die if you stay with him." It was also reported he pulled my father aside and said, "If you continue beating her, you'll kill her." I imagine the age that I heard this was nine, the same year I started writing, the same year I started acting out in school. It was embedded in my memories, along with a blue suitcase my stepmother threatened to pack and leave with, along with the purple bruises and her saying, "Don't let this happen to you, get out of here and get an education! Your father doesn't care if you work in that factory just like him."

Surprisingly, and despite my own struggles, I always did manage to get an education. Her words stayed with me along with imprints from a belt buckle she hit me with, along with raised scratches and red marks on my wrists from fingernails, and the accusations: "You're destructive." "You father's a nigger and so are you." "If your father and I had a baby she'd be light skinned with curly hair." "Your mother didn't want you." "If it weren't for me, you'd be sent back to an adoption agency." All of this was hammered and nailed into my head, without me having anyone to listen or tell. What happened to my stepmother I vowed would never happen to me, but it did—in what I did to myself, the type of women I chose, people I allowed into my life. Somehow I believed that people's image of me and their approval of me was more important than my own, of myself. I was repeatedly in dangerous situations, repeatedly the subject of rumors, mob, gang and high school types of violence. I was always in situations where I got burnt alive while people looked on impassively, or I was the target of entitled perpetrators who acted alone, the last of which was some guy who asked for my help on a project and then, after bleeding me for information proceeded to tell me, "Your face has changed, you're getting old." I never said anything about the fact that he wore hats because he was going completely bald, but hey whatever. When I told a therapist once of things said to me at random, she said, "You're empowering them." I imagine she was talking about my venting and my shows of vulnerability to the wrong people. There were all kinds of ways they figured out to lure me—kindness, money, attention, a performance; as soon as I entered, I was undermined. Their abuse manifested in going into rooms where, even though they knew me and my spirit was great, they pretended I wasn't there, or they refused to invite me to commune and to break bread.

I heard myself recently crying into the phone talking to a therapist, "After all of my life," I said, "not one person who has performed an egregious act has ever returned to me and said, 'You're right' or 'I'm sorry,'" to offer a crumb of humanity by way of acknowledgement. These are all people seen on the frontlines of marches, or on Facebook and Twitter pages adamant about the injustice of another cop killing an unarmed Black man or woman; women and Lesbians famous for espousing feminist principles; academics on the forefront of human rights work; people who showed up and said they were lovers and friends but couldn't offer another woman, a dark skinned Black woman, a Lesbian, a crumb of humanity and don't see that as political. I started a poem recently I couldn't finish, "It happens in the news, but in my life also / One more dirty disgusting beating, no one accounts for." Audre Lorde once said, "If I were a white male, I'd be rich and famous for my work." I thought at the time how petty, why would she go there? This is until my own hair began to sprout grey without still having ever known real freedom or justice. Nelson Mandela said in his autobiography *Long Walk to Freedom* that he felt as if at 60 or 70, when he'd just left prison, his life had just begun. Sometimes on the horizon, particularly in my life now, through therapy and art and new relationships, there are glimmers of freedom. At the same time, every trust of mine has been betrayed; I've experienced so many losses like bodies stacked into mass graves. I wrote once about slaves being afraid of freedom, but many, at the onset of hard won emancipation, were just too tired. Scholar Kevin Bales wrote that after emancipation, slaves were dumped into a fragile economy with no support. I myself imagine they, the slaves, just couldn't light any more candles. They'd seen too much. There were too many crisscrossed scars on their hearts, hands, necks, and backs—too many pieces cut off. The language of slavery in itself is dehumanizing. I get stuck on the separations. Imagine what it's like to see someone every day, your love and theirs is rolled into one, and to never see their face or touch them again, to not even know if they are alive. For some slaves the toll was too much—seeing skin burnt, those castrated, limping, limbs made into stumps for running away, killing that continued much longer than the Rwandan massacre.

A few weeks ago, I was called to be a cohost of Queer, Art, Film at the IFC Center. The film being presented was *The Color Purple*. I watched it that night for the umpteenth time. It's like a bible for Black women, outsiders, queers. However, I was aware in this viewing of something completely different. For me the story or the focus had always been about Celie overcoming a horrendous self-esteem resulting from systemic oppression, being poor, dark, and a woman. I had also been struck previously by the Lesbian innuendo between Celie and a Blues,

Jazz, burlesque singer Shug Avery. This relationship empowers Celie. This time I saw something different. I was struck somewhere near the beginning where Celie endures a horrific separation from her biological sister. She is literally torn out of her sister's arms by her abusive husband. The scene is harrowing and again it was something slaves faced every day that is often overlooked. Earlier in the film, we had witnessed the sisters bonding in the kitchen where a learned and literate younger sister Nettie is teaching Celie to write. Suddenly I became most aware of the word sky written in black on wax paper. Celie tucks this token into her bag. When her sister is torn away by her violent, vindictive husband, she screams to her, "Write, Write." Sometimes those words are the only ones I can say to myself when I endure nightmare after nightmare, injustices and challenges—the only way I can make sense of it all is to say to myself, like Celie calling out to her sister in peril, "Write. Write."

In my own story, with my torturers there was always a flame in their eyes that danced and became animated when I was hurt or when they saw my enormous fear. They would say things like "You need so much attention," without ever acknowledging their own desperate need for attention. I could see in their eyes a story about me, even with those whom I had never spoken to or ever broken bread. It was a story I had no control of and was chiseled in stone or grew like wild fire. They were superior. On some occasions they were nice, reached out, and as soon as I grabbed the branch I was trapped, gaslighted. I hear of the dramatic end of Ntozake Shange's *For Colored Girls*, as voiced by the lady in red, played by my friend Laurie Carlos, "& Crystal who had known so lil tenderness/let Beau Willie hold the kids.../& he dropped em."

Throughout the novel that I wrote about Joe, I was always trying to kill her off. It took some time, years after, before I realized it was me. In fiction class, I created an ending where she hung herself. My classmates who had followed her on her journeys throughout years and semesters cried. Joe hung herself from a ceiling fan. She was finished. I was in London many years later, and I woke up from a dream: It spoke to me and said, "Joe is alive." "She is alive." Her death never felt true. I never worked on the novel again after that point. I was satisfied, felt I had gotten what I needed from it, the character of Joe was alive. Joe never started out as a main character. She was the lover to a very destructive alcoholic woman, Louisa. They were the only two Lesbians in a small town in a fictitious Lynchburg, Virginia. In London, Louisa, the destructive main character, faded into the background and Joe emerged as the leader and main character; all of this was unconscious. I wrote a preface then to the novel that began with Joe's departure from her family and a small community of ex-slaves. I recall Jane, my fiction teacher saying to me, "Your novel is about freedom Pam, even if it's freedom to self-destruct."

A few years back, in 2011, I had an opportunity to travel to South Africa. The journey harkened back to my activism days at the New School/Lang College. I would look out of the windows onto 12th St. in my War and Women's Writing class. We read tales of Nelson and Winnie Mandela in the anti-apartheid struggle. I learned of places like Soweto and Bloemfontein. I never imagined that one day I would stand in those actual places, that I would be standing at an actual ATM with languages like Zulu and Afrikaans. I traveled to Soweto and ate barbeque with Black dykes outside of Bishop Desmond Tutu's house. I sat across the street from the home Nelson Mandela shared with Winnie. I visited Robben

Island, also the Hector Pieterson Museum in Soweto. Later, I had an epiphany as an adult in the apartheid museum in South Africa. I've always had a strong political self. I've always been a rebel, but a bulb went off in my head when they said that the whole of the anti-apartheid war was fought so that a young Black kid could wake-up, look in the mirror and feel good about themselves. For all of my rabble-rousing, I could not do that. Everything was fought not to address the man per se, but our own self-hatred. I realized then in my 40s in the apartheid museum in South Africa, on the edge of so many movements, I had a problem.

I mean there was a precedent for this self-abandoning, this disappearing, this beating down. I remember I had a lover early in my twenties. Yes, I made mistakes as did she, but I remember everyone was her friend. When we broke up, everyone sided with her, took care of her. As it turns out she'd been trying to steal my identity and she'd succeeded. When we broke up, she befriended everyone who was my friend. Only one of my friends noticed and said, "It's strange, she's never tried talking to me before." She worked everywhere I worked. Someone else who saw the situation in retrospect said, "You needed someone." I also worked at an agency where I was beat-up and blamed while many responsibilities were placed on my shoulders. I didn't understand some things then and didn't have a language for things like fear, threat, projection, competition, racism, woman hate, and demonization. Years later, I would hear from strangers, "Oh you're the one everyone was jealous of." If I had a complaint or two about lovers, the string or continuum, what I heard myself saying at the end was, "You wouldn't listen to me, or you weren't there for me." I would hear this sentiment out of their mouths as well, if they ever took any accounting. They would say, "I don't know why, I couldn't listen to you."

I was seeing a woman, the one whom everyone took care of. She had accused me of something, holding her back, when actually I'd fought to give her her first job. At the time, I tried to explain to her who I was, and I could see she'd already built the case—a woman who had never been to my family home, who became my enemy and nemesis and who everyone protected 20 years later. I saw her recently in passing. I have no interest in her. She looks at me with tremendous and gargantuan fear. I suppose her connection to me is kept alive through fear. Anyone that I have ever met or encountered who has been her friend looks at me through a distorted lens. When I was lovers with this woman, I remember she would look at me and say, "I'm afraid of you." I never understood, but I thought because she said this there was something wrong with me, as I was 6ft 2½in and dark Black, although she was Black herself. It's been interesting to me through all of these years no one has questioned her story. There is so much projection of others' fear against dark Black people, and people wonder why tragedies like Eric Garner and Trayvon Martin happen.

In the end, I had wanted to leave the relationship but didn't know how, so I cheated. I was 26/7 years old. I could have been more honest but that was all the language I had then. Again, she'd told me at some point to date whomever I wanted, then word got around and it spread. It was like something out of *The Scarlet Letter* or medieval fiction. I was forced to wear an identifying letter. Everywhere I went someone threw rocks or a stone. Everyone, the villagers and townspeople scorned me; for years, people ran up to me, kicked and threw punches. This lasted twenty years, even though she now has kids, has had plenty of lovers and slept with everyone I ever batted an eye at. Oh, I forgot to say this courageous woman broke up with me, after a year-and-a-half, by leaving a message on my answering machine.

Some of this would be ok if these people just outright hated me, but then I saw many modeled themselves after me, used my voice, and were better at being me than me, and sometimes when I looked back or looked at them I saw FEAR.

Later, I ran into a Black Woman who was my ex-lover's friend—another person who I helped hire at a Gay and Lesbian organization. "Hi Pamela. How are you? What are you up to?" she asked. "Oh I'm writing a book," I responded.

"But Pamela, YOU'RE NOT a writer."

"Yes, I AM."

"Pamela, I said, YOU'RE NOT a writer, YOU'RE a performer," and she was furious.

Another scenario: I was at a party talking to a random stranger. "Hi, I'm Pamela. Pamela Sneed. I remember you from back in the day."

"Hi, YOU'RE NOT Pamela Sneed."

"Yes, I AM"

"No, YOU'RE NOT."

I was at a club talking to random stranger... "Oh yeah, like Pamela Sneed."

I said, "I AM Pamela Sneed."

"No, YOU'RE not Pamela Sneed."

"I AM," I insisted and I'm not violent but it could have turned into a fistfight, like in Sherman Alexie's *The Lone Ranger and Tonto*, with her holding a part of my identity hostage and me desperately trying to retrieve it.

In another scenario with a random person: "Hi Pamela, what are you doing?"

"I'm writing."

"But YOU'RE NOT a writer, my lover is a writer, but you're not, YOU'RE a performer."

Recently, I went to a party with a lover, met a Black Lesbian artist there I was happy to see, and went to hug her. She turned her face and ran up to my lover instead. They both refused to acknowledge we'd entered the party together. The Black Lesbian proceeded to introduce my lover to the host and get herself a high-powered position. Neither really acknowledged I was there. When I mentioned this to my lover, now an ex, she didn't understand the issue, said she wanted to marry me.

Let's just say I was dating a lampshade and of course the lampshade shines bright, but the way it was portrayed, the lampshade, anything, was brighter than me—the lamp or the bulb was endowed with special powers, while I was erased.

I once went to a party and said hello to a well-known poet. I don't know her really. I was leaving and happened to catch her eye while she didn't think I was looking and I saw something that looked like sheer hatred. It was disturbing, something was being attached to me and I couldn't think that I'd done anything to her or any one of these women, as I barely left my house for many years.

Another scenario: they would act as friends, come to my performances and knew that was the place I once struggled most visibly with fear, and when I looked to them for strength or a kind eye or encouragement, they would smirk, laugh, and afterwards say, "Pamela, YOU'RE not a performer. YOU'RE a writer."

In Boston, there was a story, a case that loomed large over the city for decades. It happened in the early '60s, it was about a white man who was a serial killer. He assaulted, sexually ravaged women, and then strangled them. He was known as The Boston Strangler. Sad to say, some of these people and their behavior became a way of brutalizing, then strangling me.

When I was in Junior High School I played basketball. I loved it. Because of my height I was the Center. I can recall a game in another small town: The girl's basketball team coaches were often women, and one was a tall white woman, maybe 6ft 5in. She stalked the sides of the court, yelling at her team. I had just made a basket and a few points. I was feeling high, and I recall her yelling down the court to her team, "Go get that monster." The monster she referred to was me...

In my adult life, most of these people who've mistreated me I don't know. Like the character in *Bowfinger* or the guy in the film *Her* who gets jilted by Samantha the operating system, I've discovered over and over that as a celebrity on a smaller scale, I've been having an intimate relationship with hundreds, maybe thousands of people. They got or get to tell me who I am but the flow isn't reciprocal, not that I'm interested. I suppose the case others built against me is that I was not a person to be regarded or listened to. Mine was not a good body to inhabit. I also had all those mothers to prove it, so I jumped ship, built a wall inside myself bigger than the Berlin Wall that separated East and West Germany. I stopped listening to me as well, and all of those beautiful poems I wrote, all of the students whose lives I touched immensely, all of the men and women and audiences who found their way out of darkness by seeing me, could not penetrate the wall I built between my outer and inner self. I suppose it's what a schizophrenic describes as two selves. Recently, I told a spiritual teacher about my walls. In the presence of the Orishas, Oshun and Legba and Shango and all those deities of the Middle Passage, she asked, "What are you afraid of, touching a power greater than you have ever known?" I see Audre now, an eagle, spreading the wings of her dashiki in the sky saying, "Dare to be powerful. That power you've given me is your power! Take your power!"

Someone told me this story that I repeated in my MFA thesis work, *Right to Return*: There was so much carnage from the slave ships, from people being tossed overboard, that it permanently changed the migratory patterns of sharks. Also, like slaughterhouses, the decks of slave ships were mucousy and wet with blood. Mother, Yeymaya, the Orsiha of water is here with me now and is telling me to speak. Ever since I made the plane trip to Ghana and stood at Cape Coast Castle, those ancestors, deities, have been with me. In my soul, I have waited to see them all again.

As an adult I listen sometimes to the preachers because they remind me of my grandfather's church where I grew up. Over and over I repeat to myself Michael Beckwith's phrase, "In the beginning." "In the beginning," to say we have control over our story from the start of our day. He also repeats God's biblical phrase, "Let there be light," and he means, as I learned in school from the feminists: Consciousness. Let there be light, illumination, truth, consciousness. With all the predatory food shops and clothing stores in downtown Brooklyn, those that prey on young poor Black kids, I repeat sometimes to my students what Dr. Beckwith says to remind them of purpose, "You weren't put here to shop 'til you drop." Last week I was touched when Michael Beckwith said our lives must be more than the corporations and companies using us up until we die. My favorite is from Reverend Zach a long time ago, "Give away a dollar a day to someone in need or homeless and don't ask them what they do with it. It's none of your business." One of my students, a girl from Egypt told me, that this line really impacted her. She is now more generous. To show them I am not self-righteous and that I too struggle with compassion in this technological world, I say to them, "There is a homeless man on my block, a Black man whom I see every day. Every day he asks for a quarter, but something about him irritates me, and he makes me feel like a Republican. I want to shout, 'Get a job.'" They always laugh at this. I try to be human and funny. When I catch them texting in the classroom, which is often, I ask coyly: "Oh are AT&T or Verizon giving out degrees now?" The students laugh and respond, "No." So, I'm like, "Don't get played then." When I want to impart something serious to the students and need silence, rather than tell each individually to be quiet, I imagine myself as a movie director and say, "Alright now, quiet on the set." Once, I taught a group of adults, some I didn't think liked me much, but I had an occasion to see them all in an assembly. When I opened the door, a sea of smiles spread across the room, and they shouted excitedly repeating my phrase, "Professor Sneed! Quiet on the set!"

I have had some health issues. In this, I have noticed so many of my core needs are unmet: needs for love, companionship, to be listened to, honored, and respected. As a child, I was not allowed to talk in my house. I was not allowed to express anything. I had no voice. There was no conversation about anything. I was with my stepmother often as my father worked. I was an avid reader. My favorite thing of all time was a Nancy Drew book. The series was about a young heroine who solved mysteries. There was Nancy Drew on the front cover with a flashlight peering into a cave. They were 50 cents near the cash register. I asked for that book. I felt a pang in my stomach, the way one hungers when weaning from drugs or yearns for a mother's love. My stepmother always refused, and there was no one there to see I needed that book and how important it was. I remember telling a friend in my adult life about past friends and some terrible separations. I also told this friend about Ruthie, my first mother, and not being allowed to see her after the divorce. She said, "Your friends are your parents who didn't know how important it was for you to see your mother."

Keep in mind, none of this is complaint. None of this is victimization. This is an attempt to put a story together. I am a survivor. I guess I'm developing a voice now that says you won't get it in life until you heal yourself first. Right now, I feel as if a scab has fallen off and I'm speaking from a gaping red wound, raw and unhealed.

I don't know many things about my father, what made him the way he is; he, like the story in a Nancy Drew Book, is a mystery. I have a visual image of him as a turtle with an impenetrable shell. The only thing I can think of or see etched across his chest is—*family*. In the time between divorcing Ruth and marrying my second mother, I can only describe him as the way Harriet experiences the love of her life, John Tubman. She describes him as she first saw him: a laughing man, tall and free. My father is dark, a red brown, handsome and distinguished like MLK. I do not know all of the circumstances that changed him and made him disappear. I only know the time when I was young and my tiny feet fit into his hands, like Harriet, he'd lift me up—when he, as a high school drop-out, placed a pencil and paper into my hands and gave me the tools to survive. I have an image of the day my father took me to a dead-end street with no traffic so I could practice riding a bicycle. I was 4 or 5 year old. He took the training wheels off, gave a push, ran behind as I started to pedal and fly on my own. I don't know all of why he disappeared into violence and sorrow. Some say it was after the deaths of his parents. I believe it was the instant he married his second wife. There was a conversation he and I had when I was probably about 8 years old. My cousin, a White girl adopted by marriage by my father's brother, repeatedly ran away. It broke the family, there were constant searches for her. My father in a rare display drove me to a supermarket parking lot in the small town where we lived. We had a serious talk between us. "I want you to promise me," he said, "you'll never run away." And me, not wanting to ever hurt the love of my life said, "I won't." That was our pact. The story that had been told to me as a child was that my cousin had destroyed the family by running away. Her mother, a White woman, was always crying, always searching for her. My cousin was the example of bad girl that was shown to me. But through writing the novel of Joe and Louisa and looking upon the story again as an adult, I realized the reason she'd run away is incest. She was being molested by my uncle. So, when I wrote in fiction class about the girl who became a woman, who after years of obedience finally runs away, who becomes Joe, the piss-poor bulldagger who disappears and leaves no note, it was not a poetic device. It wasn't something made up in a fiction class that sounded pretty. It was me, who after a lifetime was leaving my father. It was me, determined to survive, who would no longer be Daddy's girl. It was me, deciding not to be one of those broken women described at the outset of the novel. It was me, not wanting a life full of purple and black bruises, and being dragged by the hair, neck, or arms up and down the stairs of a tiny apartment building. Joe, in the novel sees a storm that precipitates her leaving, but really it was an earthquake, the decision to take my life into my hands. Audre Lorde told her classes at Hunter College, "Make work as if your own life or someone else's depends upon it." Mine did.

When I first wrote Joe, my fiction teacher, standing in a classroom at the New School said, "You know Pam it would have been impossible for you less than ten years ago to write a Lesbian novel with Lesbians as primary characters and not have the novel be about lesbianism." I was aghast. "I'm not going to spend my time explaining lesbianism," I said, "or writing coming out stories." It was Jane, my fiction teacher who really became my mother, a white woman married to a Black man. She always had grey hair and was in love with Tillie Olsen. She taught me everything I know. I remember the white chalk on the blackboard, her saying: "Your novel must have a timeline. If you're stuck writing, write the end."

Shortly after I'd left home at age 18, I wrote a story that I gave to Jane at the New School, three years later. It began: "Muriel lived with ghosts, visions that invaded her consciousness with clouds of the past, prophecies of the future. Mama said the ghosts came because Muriel was a Black girl and all Black girls were cursed from birth till death. Isn't that why she caused her Mama such shame and pain? Muriel was a nigger in true definition of the word, which is why Mama's friends, family, and neighborhood acquaintances would never accept her." I had no idea that

I was documenting the relationship I had with my stepmother, quoting things said to me directly. On Jane's student evaluations she said, "You're a prodigiously gifted writer." And, "Yours is some of the best student fiction I've ever read in all of my years of teaching." Sometimes I wonder, with such promise, what if I'd been white or a straight male, or a young straight Zadie Smith and my talents were nurtured and discovered? Sometimes I wonder about all the Gay and Lesbian artists and writers both pre- and post-Stonewall whose works were before their time and went un-nurtured and undiscovered.

For a few semesters I taught at a city college. I had some very memorable experiences. I remember a very skinny Black kid who came from dense poverty, stood up to introduce himself in a presentation, and said to our surprise, "This is my man." He showed a picture of a buffed up brown man literally behind bars. I was shocked because the atmosphere was homophobic, though I guessed he felt safe in my class. There was another student, a mixed race brown kid from Uganda, who announced he was Gay. "In my country, I could be killed for who I am." I also was touched by a young Black Lesbian who brought in pictures of herself and her lover. The photos proudly displayed a rainbow flag behind them. She also said in a courageous moment, "I've lost both of my parents to AIDS." I can't forget either a Black student who barely spoke, but once he got up in front of the class and talked about how he lost his only brother to gun violence. "When I got to the funeral home, my legs gave way and I couldn't walk," he said. Another student there also had a great impact on me. She was a dark Black woman, she got up for a presentation and was wearing a dress and had prominent scars around her neck. I don't know how she got them. She presented herself and her history and what an achievement it was for her to be in college, and then she almost shouted in a voice that was deeply resonant, "I don't want to be just another statistic." I realized then, in her, in that statement, was me. There was a student in a speech class I taught, a young woman, an immigrant, somehow she confided in me, and in a presentation said she been molested by her father over and over when she came to America. She was beholden to him because of her immigrant status. He destroyed her self-esteem, said she'd be nothing. So getting into college for her was quite an achievement. When she told me the story through tears, I told her, "Don't worry about the grammar or anything, we'll fix it later. Just write." She did. It was healing. Her face had changed—had more light at the end of the semester. I'd mentioned once in class I wanted to learn to drive as a birthday present to myself. On the last day of class, she pulled out a new driver's manual and gave it to me. She said, "I thought you might like this."

Yes, so the story I created about Joe was not a poetic device. I was going against everything I was taught: the church, my mother, silence, supposed tos, the sure fate for Black girls of my hue and class. I was taking up in spirit the occupation my father loved and was known for—boxing. It was me and him in the early days watching Muhammad Ali. Ali was everything to my father. Perhaps it was my father who said to me, about the contentious relationship between newscaster Howard Cosell and Muhammad Ali, "You know Cosell loved Ali." It was me who tied the black gloves on and stepped into the ring for the greatest fight—not for sport, but for my life. I'm thinking about something ridiculous, a movie I saw a long time ago called *I Am Sam* where Sean Penn plays a mentally disabled man trying to keep his daughter after the state tries to take her away. He doesn't have the means or the resources and, trial after trial, he is defeated, like all those Gay men in the '80s and early '90s lying in hospital rooms, who the world turned their backs on, surrounded by death and fear. I'm going to reference the writer Hilton Als here where he says that, after their deaths, Gay men with AIDS were being tossed out into the streets in garbage bags. In my own words, they were shrouded in cobwebs of loneliness and abandonment. In *I Am Sam*, Michelle Pfeiffer who plays Sam's lawyer goes to him in the hour of defeat and hands him back the gloves he's lost, as when the great actor Burgess Meredith says to a deflated Rocky Balboa, "I'm willing to go ten more rounds, if you can." He responds, "Yes." And all of my life, that's been me, following in the footsteps of the runaway Harriet Tubman and freedom fighters. I am like the fictitious Rocky Balboa getting up when no one wanted or expected him to, getting up when odds of surviving were slim, when the world bet against him. He was counted out time and again. It was me, who landed like the student in Kennedy airport in the dead of winter with no coat in pursuit of freedom and a better life.

And I have lost things, oh I have lost things and I am ashamed, but as Dorothy Allison once claimed in my most favorite essay, "Deciding to Live," writing was evidence of the desire to live. I suppose this is common knowledge now, and it's truth is still debatable for some, but shortly after Mandela's release from jail after serving 27 years in prison, it's said he developed Alzheimer's; his brain was all but gone, which is why he only served one term as president. They hid him away, got him to raise his hand for press purposes. For a man who spent his life fighting for freedom and justice, he saw so little of it.

In Jane's fiction class we were given an assignment to read and write about Mary Shelley's *Frankenstein.* I compared myself as a Black Lesbian peering through windows into a society where I did not belong. As an adult, I remember the parallel and having occasions now to look or peer into the windows of the society where I do not belong. I've seen that some are predators, others prominent members of the Gay and Lesbian community who hold high positions and are deeply misogynistic, not out to their families, all extremely narcissistic and entitled and they all have support, places to rest and lay their head. Many possess the negative qualities they've attached to me which couldn't be further from who I am.

The third biggest part of my identity was/is becoming a teacher, a healer. Sometimes I feel so strong in this like I can move my hand and broken things are made whole: Like when I taught many years ago in an upscale summer program and an 11-year-old debutante declared, as feminist anthem, "I hate pink."

And...

—The other in downtown Brooklyn, a student who took a speech final, and waited until everyone had left the room, pulled a bouquet of white tulips out of his bag and said, "You changed me."

—The other an older adult Black woman student at an art school who said recently, "You gave me freedom. I didn't know how much over the years my voice had become merely a whisper."

—And then the Chinese girl from a conservative Chinese background with a traditional name declaring, unprompted, in my class about poetry and social movements, "My research paper will be on Audre Lorde. She was a Black Lesbian, one breasted Feminist mother, warrior poet."

—The other student was from a fancy conservative school, a Black girl who after one semester with me came to class with a cleanly shaved head after a lifetime of perms.

There are several Black women who have come up to me recently at readings, by referral, or randomly. They cry. They ask me to teach them. They say they just need to know I exist. Sometimes I tell my students, "I'm Harriet Tubman and I don't like to lose passengers." They laugh. Sometimes, I think at the beginning of every semester, I am Noah loading the ark and my job is to carry them through the storm, deliver them to another shore safely. It's a game of Survivor, and if they ever go out as I did on a rooftop so many years ago in a drug-fueled haze on the Lower East Side trying to decide whether or not to live, I pray that something I said to them in class will be a message in that little black box, like the one kept on planes in times of emergency, the one that's in every soul. As an adult I've had an idea to write a children's book about a hero called Poetry. I want to teach children how in dire times Poetry can save them and they can create her. In my little black box, it was Poetry who saved me. It was Poetry who showed up on the rooftop, loaded me onto her wings when I was in a drug-fueled haze on the Lower East Side and told me, "Don't Jump. You have so many reasons to live," Poetry, who like Harriet Tubman shouted to her passengers on the Underground Railroad, "Keep Going!"

One of the things that makes me an effective teacher is that I'm not someone who can watch or stand on the sidelines. I'm someone, using that great boxing metaphor, who gets in the ring with students. I myself have battled and seen so much fear. Maybe like in the sci-fi series *Dr. Who*, fear is an old foe, like Sidney Poitier and Tony Curtis we are lifelong partners dancing together. We know each other intimately. Fear: I've seen it faces of dying friends. I've seen it displace and cripple people. I've seen otherwise healthy people suffer paralysis. Like Harriet, I am no stranger to fear. I worked with a Black guy recently, he was a visual artist. He spoke very philosophically about making a graphic novel, one that could be displayed on the walls. There were all sorts of pictures on the wall, and one was of a runaway slave. He didn't seem so grounded in his project and finally I had reached my rope's end with the conversation which is unusual for me with students and I blurted out of the runaway slave, "You have to understand that it's not a random image, that runaway slave on the wall is you." We both fell back shocked and enlightened.

And I have this to hold against myself: the ways I have made or make myself invisible or disappear.

All of this is significant because the other day I went out for a walk, which I try to do every day as much as I can. There was a hurricane in New York, and after being confined, a lot of people were out on the streets cleaning up. My walk is a long neighborhood route far from my house. Every day I take this route, I pass an old White man in a wheelchair who sits outside. Every day I say hello. I dismissed him as an old window-watcher type. This time he yells out to me:

"How are you doing Professor Sneed?"

I gasped.

"How did you know who I am?" I asked him astonished, thinking I'd succeeded in being invisible.

He laughed and said, "They say I'm the mayor here."

I want to tell you a perfect story, about how I overcame all, am the heroine who triumphs over all. But mine is not a perfect story. Like the hundreds of thousands of runaway slaves, I have gotten my foot caught in many traps, gotten stuck somewhere between freedom and slavery. I drag my manacles. I suffer. To survive, there have been many parts cut off.

In my book of poetry *KONG*, I call for tribunals against the Bush administration for what it did in Katrina, for its false wars in Iraq and Afghanistan, but I think there should also still be tribunals for slavery, crimes against humanity. The founding fathers should be stripped of their titles and if statues are made, their heads must be bowed in shame. I think there should be ongoing tribunals for crimes exacted by the medical system and government against women, and for what was done to Gay men and their families and friends during the '80s and early '90s AIDS crisis. I have this fantasy too, that one day I could stand amongst some of my peers, former lovers, and friends and bare my chest—part of what I am doing now—and show the crisscrossed scars on my heart, imprints left from belt buckles and finger nails, rumors, mobs, gang violence, and the lasting scars from solitary confinement.

I started a poem that is lost; the first few lines began:

> *Never thought I would be here*
> *To call forth my own people, the Rainbow tribe*
> *As they did in South Africa, Bosnia, Rwanda*
> *To not talk about what the world did to us*
> *But what we did to each other*

There is a woman I loved once, we were out in a rainstorm, her socks and shoes were drenched. She looked at me and said "take me home." I knew this was an important point in our relationship. I took her home and sat her on the edge of the bathtub and stripped off her shoes and socks and ran warm water over her feet. Afterwards, I wrapped her feet in a warm towel. I admired that she could say it. Maybe now, though it's just a baby step, I am taking myself home.

I can offer this as epilogue:

Joe does return to Lynchburg, Virginia as an aged blues singer. She has spent years in a time capsule as a runaway traveling an unlit road. She meets many orphans and misfits like herself.

The last part is unwritten and I'm not sure how it can be achieved, but upon return she is a wild, sold-out success. When she actually appears and opens on stage she is no longer Joe, but has morphed into the character of Big Mama Thornton.

Postscript

More often these days, there are occasions when I get such a strong sense of how powerful I am: I feel tall, the full height of 6ft 2½in, looming large. My power comes to me like a wind, a gust, a deep breath released; it lifts me up. I felt it most recently in a classroom during a writing class. I was talking to my students about overcoming fear. I could feel and see the students laugh and be serious and completely follow me. I was making a joke about struggling with fear. I told them about a character inside of me, which should be a monologue in a stand-up routine. I call this character my crack addict. I'm not for shaming drug addicts. Everyone in America is one. I always say if we want a revolution in this country, take away sugar and coffee, there would be an immediate uprising. I firmly believe US attitudes towards addicts need to change. There are times when I say to my students, the only people on television who visibly have no rights left are addicts. They are policed, murdered, generally anything can happen to them. This discussion comes in the context of teaching human rights and Kafka's *Metamorphosis*. Who are the bugs of society? I ask. Anyway, as I explain to these current students in a writing class, I have a character inside of me and I never know when they or she will appear. Usually it's during a theater audition, everything is going well until the crack addict appears. She hates auditions, can't take cues, can't memorize, and says all the wrong things. She also makes sudden appearances when I'm on a date. The students laugh as I tell them this and they identify. Laughter has a way of making fear less powerful. There's another point I wanted to make that I was saving for my memoir titled "My Soul Went With Her," which I've pretty much completed in its first or second incarnation. The memoir is titled after Winnie Mandela's memoir about Nelson Mandela written during the height of the apartheid era. When he went underground, was jailed, incarcerated, she says, "part of my soul went with him." My memoir is about freedom fighters and runaways slaves and the fable of those who could fly.

My memoir ends in Brooklyn when I'm walking past Madiba restaurant with my White South African friend who has two mixed-race sons. We are talking about South Africa, which is where I met her. She says, "My sons are now part of the generation called Born Frees." I was so excited. I had never heard this information. It warmed me to know that after so much struggle and pain there could be a new generation called Born Frees.

Hearing this after all the years I've fought and felt grounded, I lift up like MLK and DiCaprio's character on a mountaintop.

Like the girl/woman on a rooftop in trouble who is loaded onto the wings of and rescued by a hero called POETRY

I start to fly and

I can see everything.

Acknowledgments

Special Thanks to Rachel Levitsky, Gregg Bordowitz, Natasha Shapiro, Amy Scholder, Karen Finley, Dorothy Allison, and Tracie Morris.

Shout outs to Denniston Hill, Brenda Shaughnessy, Louis Parascandola, Rachael Guynn Wilson, Ellen Goldin, Shelley Marlow, Kathleen Laziza, and Michael Bennett.

From the forthcoming collection: "Anna Mae, For Me, Tina Turner and All Black Women Survivors."

About the Author

Pamela Sneed is a New York-based poet, writer and performer. She is author of *Imagine Being More Afraid of Freedom Than Slavery, KONG and Other Works* and a chaplet, *Gift,* by Belladonna. She has been featured in the *New York Times Magazine*, *The New Yorker*, *Time Out*, *BOMB*, *VIBE*, and on the cover of *New York Magazine*. She has appeared in *Art Forum*, *The Huffington Post* and *Hyperallergic*. In 2017, She was a Visiting Critic at Yale and Columbia University. She is a Visiting Professor at Columbia University's School of the Arts for 2017/18. She is online faculty at Chicago's School of the Art Institute teaching Human Rights and Writing Art and has also been a Visiting Artist at SAIC in the MFA summer low-res program. She has performed at the Whitney Museum, Brooklyn Museum, Poetry Project, NYU and Pratt Universities, Smack Mellon Gallery, The High Line, and was an artist- in- residence at Pratt University, Denniston Hill and Poet-Linc, Lincoln Center Education. She directed a final showcase at Lincoln Center Atrium. Her collage work appeared in Avram Finklestein's *FOUND* at The Leslie Lohman Museum in 2017. Her work appears in Nikki Giovanni's *The 100 Best African American Poems*.